The Glisten Trilogy Coloring Book

Story By Debby Hackbarth

Illustrations by Carter Hlavin, Debby Hackbarth, and Jonah Hackbarth

Dedication:

To my family for their love, encouragement, and advice.

To my grandchildren for their inspiration.

To John for his constant support.

Thanks:

To Carter and Jonah for their gifted artwork.

To Jim for his editing help.

The Glisten Trilogy Coloring Book

Aquamarine stood by to watch his mate's egg hatch. His body glowed in hues of blue, green, and aqua.

The beautiful egg was a sight to behold! It
glistened in hues of green, yellow, and blue.

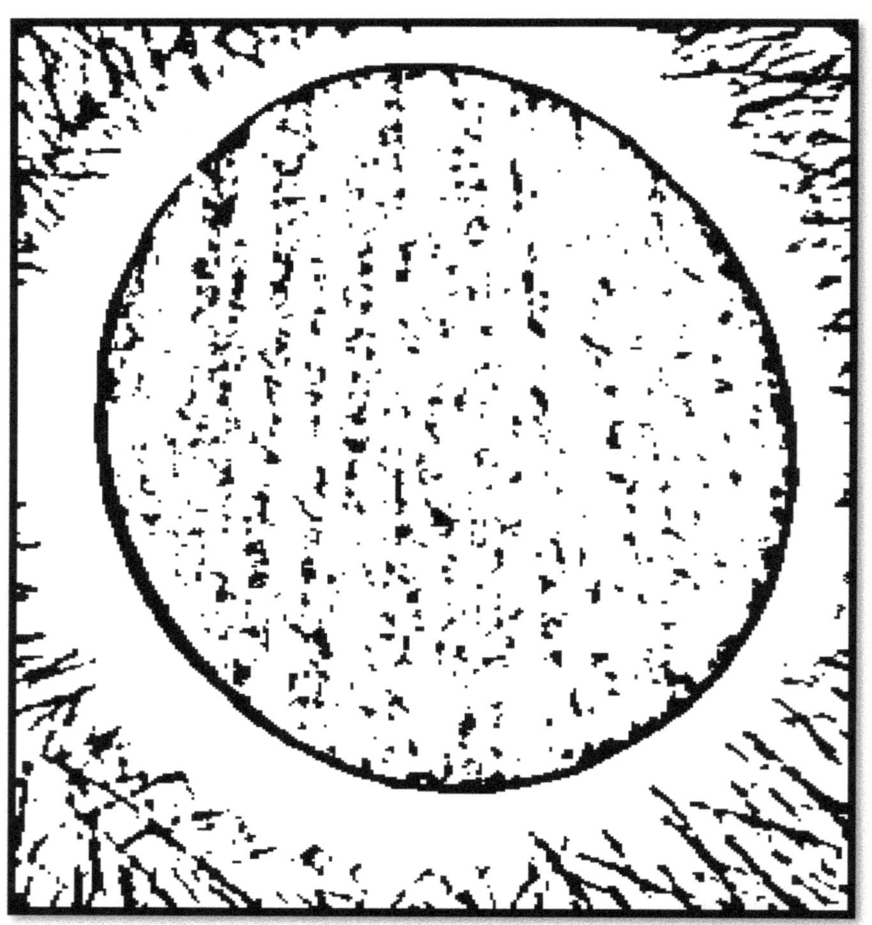

The tiny Fairhope dragon, Glisten, hatched a year early! Her blue head poked out from the brilliant egg.

Glisten's favorite food was the pink-colored popcorn, or grass, shrimp from Week's Bay.

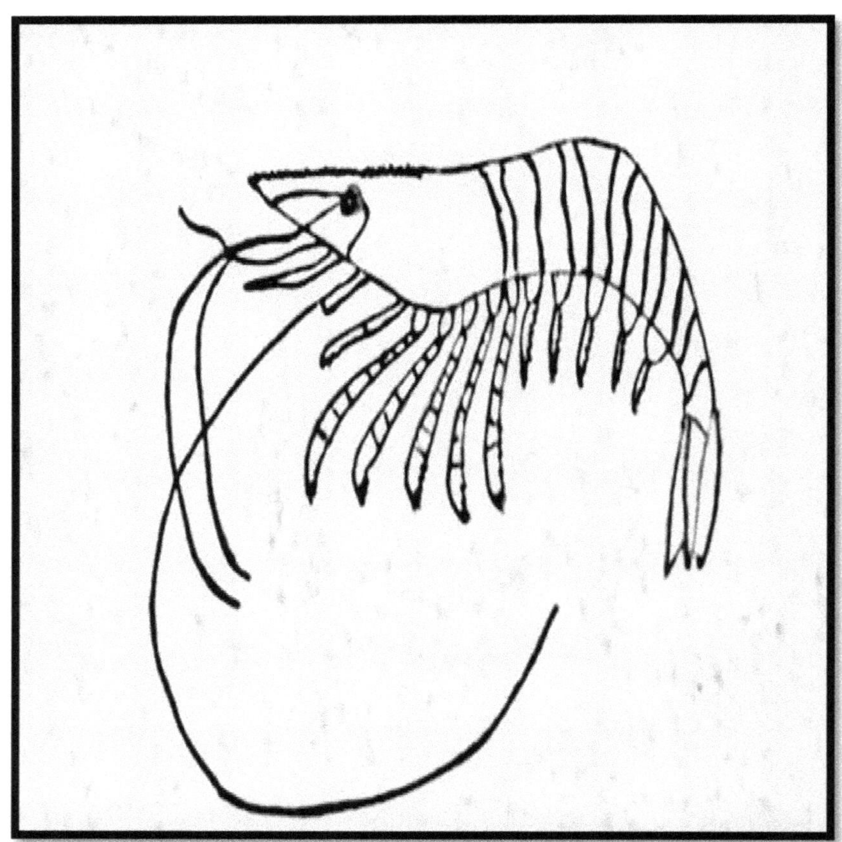

The dragon family lived inside an old grey barn north of Week's Bay. Because they saw humans in the area, the three dragons left for their safety.

A Fairhope family, Susy, Gary, Katarina, and Kaleb, moved to a farm close to the dragons' barn. They loved using their neighbor's green tractor.

Twins, Katarina and Kaleb, thrived in the warm Alabama climate where they spend time with their grandparents.

Paramedics tried unsuccessfully to save Susy and Gary when they became ill. The orphaned twins moved in with their neighbor, Mariposa.

One sunny morning, Glisten decided to find where she was hatched. She flew from Wolf's Bay west to Week's Bay.

Glisten slept in the yellow straw. When Kaleb heard a noise in the straw, he hid behind a large dark bag.

Glisten woke up and saw Katarina dancing into the barn. The dragon flew out and almost crashed into Katarina.

Like Glisten's parents, the twins named the dragon Glisten. Her blue and green colors glistened in the sunlight.

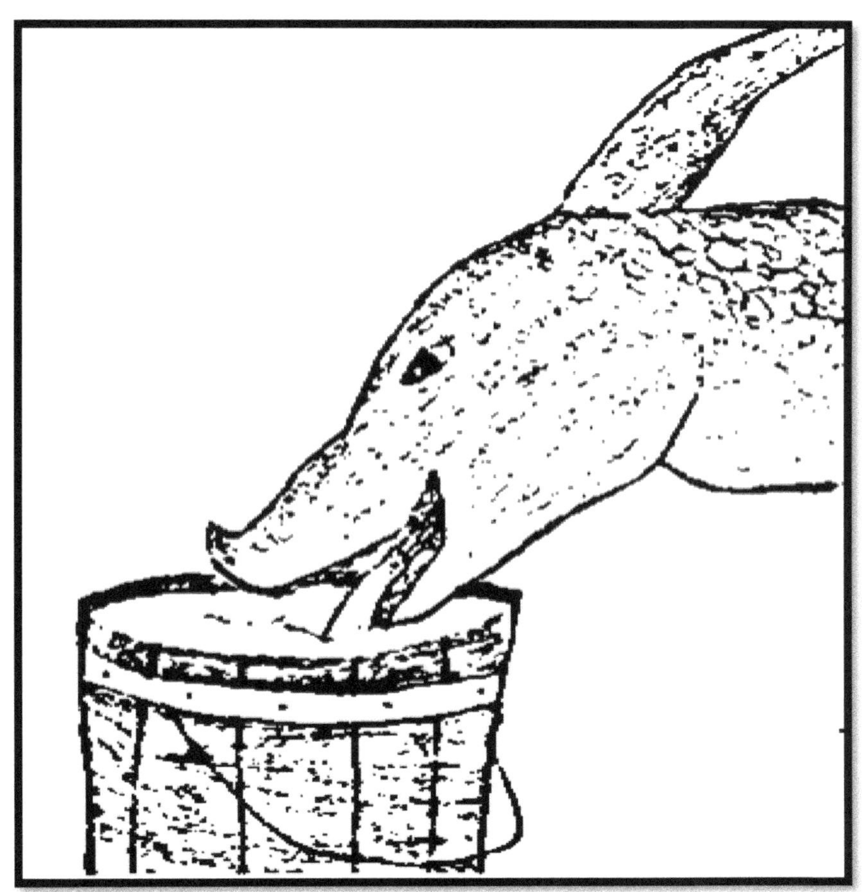

Katarina taught Glisten how to drink milk from a large bucket.

Mariposa, Katarina, and Kaleb learned to ride Glisten.

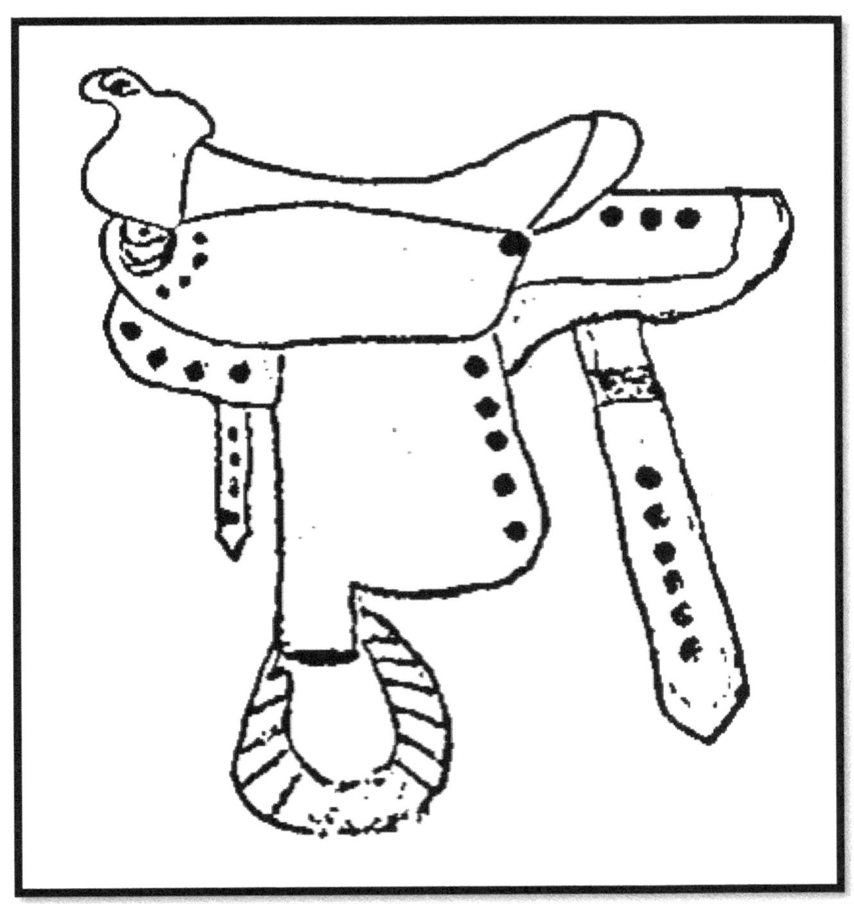

Kaleb fashioned handsome brown and tan saddles. Now riding Glisten would be safer.

Katarina and Kaleb loved living with their guardian, Mariposa.

After Glisten and Mariposa flew away,
neighbors, Ruby and William, watched over the
twins.

Ruby and William had three teens, Carter, Lucy, and Jonah.

The two adults and five teens headed out to search for Glisten and Mariposa. The ladies could wear the floral jackets Katarina made on their quest.

After many days, the hikers found Mariposa and Glisten by Wolf Bay. The twins were so excited to see their best friend!

Kaleb found a dragon community by Reeder Lake. Glisten loved to use dragon language with her new green and multi-colored friends.

Glisten chose Ember as her mate. His body shimmered in shades of orange, red, and blue.

Happily, another set of twins entered the story.
Their colors mirrored the colors of Ember and
Glisten's bodies – shades of green and blue.

Glisten and Ember lived happily ever after in the fields and woods of Alabama.

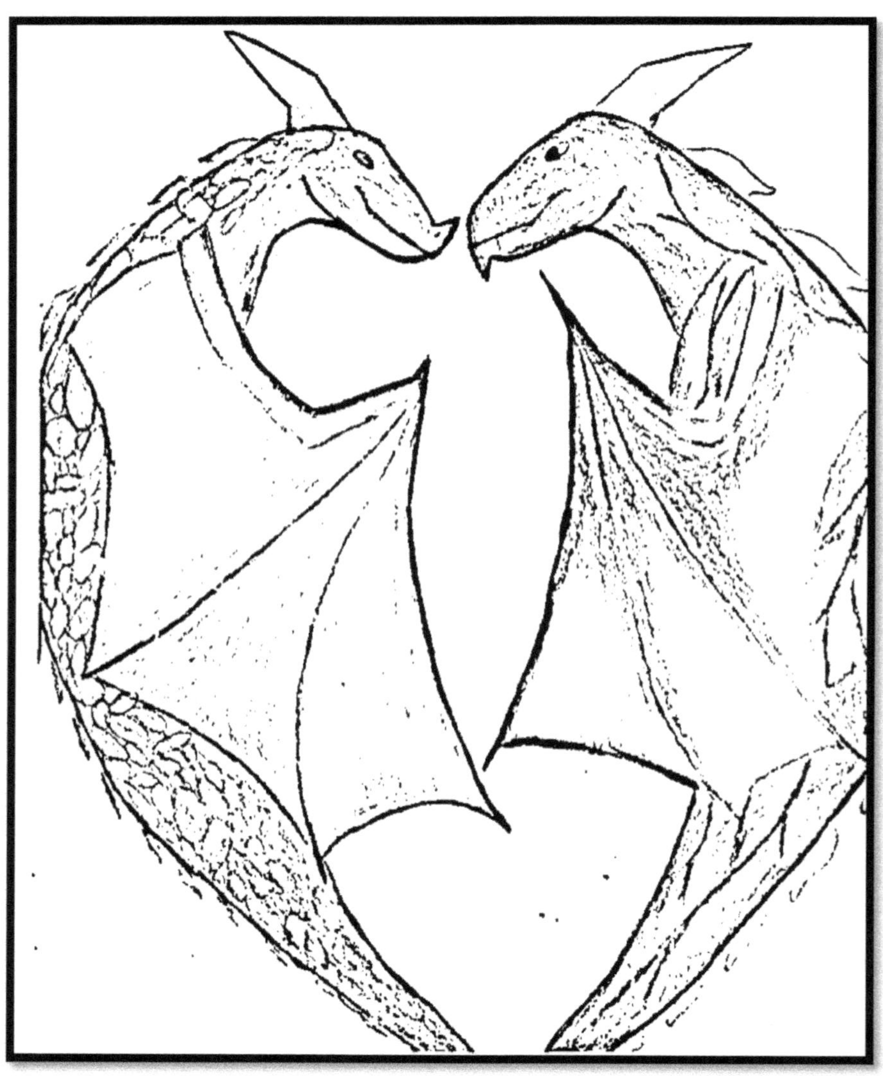